HOW GEORGIE RADBOURN SAVED BASEBALL

DAVID SHANNON

SCHOLASTIC INC.

New York Toronto London Auckland Sydney
Mexico City New Delhi Hong Kong

TO THE DITTMAN FAMILY
AND MY WIFE, HEIDI

This book was originally published in hardcover by
The Blue Sky Press in 1994.

ISBN 0-590-47411-1

Copyright © 1994 by David Shannon
All rights reserved. Published by Scholastic Inc.

SCHOLASTIC and associated logos are trademarks and/or registered
trademarks of Scholastic Inc.

12 11 10 9 8 7 6 5 4 3   04 05

Printed in the United States of America   08

Design by Kathleen Westray

First Scholastic Trade paperback printing, April 2000

The paintings in this book were executed in acrylic.
The text type was set in Scotch by
WLCR New York, Inc., New York, New York.
Color separations were made by Color Dot Graphics,
St. Louis, Missouri.

IT WAS WINTER IN AMERICA when Georgie Radbourn was born. It was *always* winter. Year after year, snow covered the factories, fields, and houses from New York to St. Louis to Los Angeles. The entire country was freezing cold. For this was a time when baseball had been declared illegal. And the strange thing was that without baseball, spring didn't come, and the snow didn't melt, and the sky stayed gray.

But it hadn't always been like this. . . .

LONG, LONG AGO, MANY YEARS BEFORE GEORGIE WAS BORN, THERE HAD BEEN FOUR SEASONS in America — spring, summer, autumn, and winter. Every April the nation had celebrated spring with the opening of baseball season. Baseball was the national pastime, the ballparks were packed, and folks rooted for their favorite teams all summer long.

But one year a young ballplayer named Boss Swaggert was in a terrible slump. Fans who once had cheered for him now booed when he came to bat. And the more the crowds jeered, the meaner Boss Swaggert's heart became.

One day Boss was at the plate, and the bases were loaded. This was his chance to win the game and be the hero. In came the pitch, but with a colossal swing, the mighty Boss struck out — *again*.

The fans booed him mercilessly. "You bum!" they yelled. "Get outta here!"

Boss stormed off the field. He vowed he would never play baseball again. And someday, if he had his way, no one would.

Years passed, and Boss Swaggert worked hard and became a very rich man. But even with all his money, he never forgot that rotten day at the ballpark so long ago. He thought about it day and night. And he cooked up a plan to rid America of baseball forever.

Boss used his money to buy radio and television stations and newspaper companies and magazines. Every day folks read about the evils of baseball in his papers, or heard about them on his radio and TV shows.

He made great windy speeches to big noisy crowds.

"Millions of people are starving while ballplayers are making millions!" he bellowed. "Let's tear down the ballparks and build factories instead. Then everyone will have jobs!"

Pretty soon Boss Swaggert had the whole country believing that life in America would be good only if baseball were outlawed once and for all.

Then Boss bought lots of expensive presents for all the politicians. His power grew and grew. Finally, he even managed to have the President arrested for "Conspiracy to Commit Baseball." The President couldn't deny he'd thrown out the first ball of the season. Boss Swaggert then declared himself Chief Executive Officer of America, and outlawed baseball completely.

Right off the bat, Boss threw all the ballplayers into the freezing cold Candlestick Prison, and he confiscated all the baseball equipment.

Next he outlawed the shape of the baseball diamond, and even made baseball sayings illegal. People were locked up just for calling someone a "screwball," or for saying a movie was a "hit."

Out came the bulldozers, down came the ballparks, and up went a new set of factories. Boss put everyone over the age of eight to work in those factories, and he gave them all paychecks each week. He formed a gang of thugs called the Factory Police, and he used them to spy on the public.

Now, Ebbet and Mary Radbourn were simple folks, and like everyone else, they were happy at first. They agreed when people said, "Boss Swaggert's right. It's only a game. Who needs it when we can all have more money instead?"

But then April rolled around . . . and May . . . and June . . . and still the weatherman said, "More unseasonably cold temperatures and continued snow flurries tomorrow." Trees stayed bare, flowers didn't bloom, birds didn't sing, and winter went on and on — even in places like San Diego, where it had never been cold. And as icy months turned into freezing years, even those jobs everyone had been so crazy about didn't seem to accomplish much, except to make Boss Swaggert richer. Without baseball — and spring — to lift their spirits, the people became tired and sad.

Ebbet and Mary hoped that the coming birth of their child would bring a little light into their lives.

Georgie Radbourn was born in April during what Boss's newspapers called "the Mother of All Snowstorms." Ebbet and Mary were very proud of their baby boy, but as he grew older and began to talk, they discovered something truly odd about him: Every time he opened his mouth to speak, forbidden sayings of baseball popped out.

"Batter up!" he would shout, followed by, "Hum that apple; shoot that pea!" What he meant was: "Good morning! What's for breakfast?"

Ebbet and Mary didn't know what to do. Secret trips to sympathetic doctors produced no answers.

"It's a freak of nature," the doctors said, scratching their heads.

Georgie tried to hold his tongue. His parents were afraid of the Factory Police, and he made the neighbors nervous. But as time passed, a growing number of people began to feel that there was something special about the boy, as if his strange affliction might somehow save them from their misery, and they hid him from the eyes and ears of Boss Swaggert's men.

With winter everywhere and baseball just a memory, the only fun left for children in America was throwing snowballs. Georgie and his friends found that the Factory Police made the most thrilling targets.

"Hit 'em where they ain't!" Georgie yelled, and his friends let loose a snowy barrage. Then they ran. Georgie was the best. He was super fast and deadly accurate, and he could throw snowballs that curved around the corners of buildings, catching the cops off guard.

All too soon, it was Georgie's ninth birthday, and he was ordered to report for work at the factory. His parents panicked. How could they keep his baseball talk a secret?

Finally they thought of a plan.

"We'll wrap your face in bandages," Mary said, "and we'll tell the supervisor you had an accident with the stove."

Ebbet tried to console his son. "It won't be any fun," he told Georgie, "but it's a lot better than being caught by the Factory Police."

The plan worked fine for three weeks. But one day, Georgie was working near his mother when the deadly gears of the factory machinery caught her skirt and started to pull her in. Without thinking, Georgie tore off his bandages and yelled a warning.

"No hitter!" was what came out.

His mother turned just in time to wrench free, but in the next instant, Georgie was surrounded by the Factory Police.

"TRIAL OF THE CENTURY" screamed the newspaper headlines, and the whole country was abuzz with rumors, hopes, and whispers. No one as young as Georgie had ever been arrested before. Adding to the excitement was the news that Boss Swaggert had declared himself the judge — and the jury!

On the day of the trial, crowds overflowed down the prison courthouse steps, and people filled the streets for blocks and blocks. The courtroom was in an uproar.

Every time Georgie opened his mouth to plead innocent, something illegal came out. "Line drive back through the box!" he shouted. And, "Going, going, gone!"

Judge Swaggert ordered the boy gagged, and he slammed his gavel on the bench.

By now the crowd was chanting, "Georgie! Georgie!"

"Order, order!" Boss shouted, his face as red as a hot dog.

Georgie's lawyer approached the judge. "Your Honor," she began, "my client is very sorry, and he would like to offer a proposal to settle this matter quickly."

The courtroom became quiet.

"My client proposes a simple contest of wits and skill."

"Oh?" said Boss, warming to the challenge. "And what might be the nature of this contest?"

The lawyer hesitated. "A — pardon my language — a baseball game."

A gasp rippled through the crowd.

"If Georgie Radbourn can strike you out on three pitches, you will free him and once again make baseball the national pastime."

At this, a roar went up from the crowd, the likes of which had not been heard since the old ballparks were bulldozed.

Boss Swaggert snickered. *This pip-squeak couldn't whiff me in a million years,* he thought. *I used to be a famous hitter.*

"I accept the offer," he announced with a sly grin. "And if I should manage a hit" — he paused to lean so far over the bench that his pockmarked potato nose was inches from the boy's face — "I will cut out his treasonous tongue and throw him and his parents into prison for the rest of their lives. Let's get on with it!" he roared.

With that, the whole mob spilled out the side doors and into the snowy prison yard.

The crowd settled in on either side, and foul lines were drawn in the snow. A bat and ball were brought out from the great piles of equipment that had been locked up for years.

Georgie was filled with wonder at the sight of his first real baseball. He turned it over in his hand and smelled the horsehide. He felt as if he'd found a part of himself that had always been missing.

As the big man and the small boy took up their positions, the people, inspired by Georgie, began to root openly against Boss.

"Give him the high hard one, kid!"

"Backdoor the bum!"

It felt good to shout out those words, to root for their favorite ballplayer again.

Boss dug in, wiggled his big, round backside, and cocked a huge eyebrow. Georgie glanced at his mother, went into his windup, and let the ball fly.

Boss could hear the hum of the ball's stitches as he swung wildly and missed.

"Steeerike one!" bellowed the umpire, and the crowd exploded.

Boss Swaggert was livid. He rolled up his sleeves and glared out at the small pitcher.

"Let's see that again!" he hollered.

Georgie wound up and fired another fastball, but this time Boss was ready. He swung hard, and there was the smell of burning wood as bat met ball.

The crowd groaned as the ball soared high and deep toward the prison wall.

But wait! It was curving . . . curving . . .

"Foul ball — steeerike two!"

Boss Swaggert grinned. This wouldn't end like that game so many years ago — he had this kid's number! He leaned out toward Georgie, stuck out his ugly tongue, and made a chopping motion with his hand.

Georgie was unruffled. He stared in at Boss, expressionless. Again he wound up, and again he delivered the pitch — straight, true, and fast.

Boss cocked his bat and stepped into the pitch.

In unison the crowd yelled, "Swing!" and swing Boss did, as hard as he could.

But this time, as the ball rocketed toward home, it curved like no one had ever seen, even in the glory days. It curved as if it were rounding the corner of a building.

Boss missed it by a mile, and the force of his swing blew him out of his shirt and his tie, out of his pin-striped pants, and even out of his size-fourteen wing-tip shoes!

"Steeerike three! You're outta there!" howled the umpire.

And then a wonderful thing happened. . . .

As the crowd leaped to its feet and Boss crumpled in a heap on home plate, the steely cover of clouds broke open, and the sun came streaming through like a ball club taking the field to start a new season. The snow melted away to reveal a shimmering green baseball diamond.

The people swarmed onto the field and lifted Georgie to their shoulders. Long-hidden bats and balls were pulled out of attics and out from behind stairways.

"Play ball!" shouted Georgie. And everybody did.

And so, today, there is baseball in America once again. There is still winter, but now there is spring and summer, and autumn, too. And there are still jobs to do. Only now, some of them are at the ballpark.

PEANUTS